THE HAUNTED HOUSE THAT JACK BUILT

THE HAUNTED HOUSE THAT JACK BUILT

Helaine Becker

illustrated by David Parkins

Scholastic Canada Ltd.
Toronto New York London Auckland Sydney
Mexico City New Delhi Hong Kong Buenos Aires

Scholastic Canada Ltd.
604 King Street West, Toronto, Ontario M5V 1E1, Canada

Scholastic Inc.
557 Broadway, New York, NY 10012, USA

Scholastic Australia Pty Limited
PO Box 579, Gosford, NSW 2250, Australia

Scholastic New Zealand Limited
Private Bag 94407, Botany, Manukau 2163, New Zealand

Scholastic Children's Books
Euston House, 24 Eversholt Street, London NW1 1DB, UK

Library and Archives Canada Cataloguing in Publication
Becker, Helaine, 1961-
    The haunted house that Jack built / by Helaine Becker ; illustrated by David Parkins.
ISBN 978-0-545-98539-0
    I. Parkins, David II. Title.
III. Title: This is the house that Jack built.
PS8553.E295532H38 2010   jC813'.6   C2010-900162-1

6 5 4 3   Printed in Singapore   46   13 14 15 16

For the scarily awesome Jennifer MacKinnon.
And to my sister, Jackie, who thinks this book
should have been called
The Haunted House that Jackie Built.
— H.B.

For Paul and Wendy,
for Halloween parties in the barn and
New Year bonfires in the snow.
— D.P.

This is the house that Jack built.

3

This is the stew
That cooled in the house that Jack built.

This is the ghost,
That sampled the stew
That cooled in the house that Jack built.

This is the ghoul,
That scared the ghost,
That sampled the stew
That cooled in the house that Jack built.

This is the mummy,
That chased the ghoul,
That scared the ghost,
That sampled the stew
That cooled in the house that Jack built.

This is the beast with the pointy horn,
That tossed the mummy,
That chased the ghoul,
That scared the ghost,
That sampled the stew
That cooled in the house that Jack built.

This is the fairy all forlorn,
That froze the beast with the pointy horn,
That tossed the mummy,
That chased the ghoul,
That scared the ghost,
That sampled the stew
That cooled in the house that Jack built.

This is the count, on the prowl until morn,
That bit the fairy all forlorn,
That froze the beast with the pointy horn,
That tossed the mummy,
That chased the ghoul,
That scared the ghost,
That sampled the stew
That cooled in the house that Jack built.

This is the skeleton, tattered and torn,
That teased the count, on the prowl until morn,
That bit the fairy all forlorn,
That froze the beast with the pointy horn,
That tossed the mummy,
That chased the ghoul,
That scared the ghost,
That sampled the stew
That cooled in the house that Jack built.

This is the witch, her wickedness sworn,
That rattled the bones of the skeleton torn,
That teased the count, on the prowl until morn,
That bit the fairy all forlorn,
That froze the beast with the pointy horn,
That tossed the mummy,
That chased the ghoul,
That scared the ghost,
That sampled the stew
That cooled in the house that Jack built.

This is the monster popping the corn,
That he gave to the witch, still wicked but worn . . .

23

And the rattling skeleton, tattered and torn,
And the love-struck count, done with fearing the morn,
And the fabulous fairy no longer forlorn,
And the two-headed beast with the crumpled up horn,
The fearsome mummy,
The ghastly ghoul,
The spooky ghost . . .

And they all ate stew —
And their trick-or-treats too —
At the Halloween do,
That was held in the house that Jack built!

RECIPE FOR HALLOWEEN SKELETON STEW

By Verta Bray

TAKE A SMIDGE
OF CARTILAGE

ADD SOME HINTS
OF LIGAMENTS

STIR THE STEW
WITH BONES AND GLUE

BOIL HARD
IN A GRAVEYARD

AND WHEN IT'S DONE
YOU'D BETTER RUN!!!!!